How to Become a Superhero
Somos8 Series

© Text: Davide Calì and Luis Amavisca, 2022
© Illustrations: Gómez, 2022
© Edition: NubeOcho, 2022
www.nubeocho.com · hello@nubeocho.com

Text Editing: Caroline Dookie, Rebecca Packard

First Edition: September, 2022
ISBN: 978-84-18133-29-9
Legal Deposit: M-5814-2022

Printed in Portugal.

All rights reserved.

HOW TO BECOME A SUPERHERO

Davide Calì
Illustrated by Gómez

nubeOCHO

So you want to be a...

SUPERHERO!

Well, first, you need to work on your...

SUPERHERO LOOK!

A cape is cool for a dramatic entrance.

But it can also be **A PROBLEM** if you trip on it.

THE COLOR OF YOUR COSTUME

All **BLACK?** Wow, very sophisticated!

All **WHITE?** Elegant but hard to keep clean.

ALL RED? Cool!

What about **RED AND BLUE?** A classic look.

How about trying something different? **GREEN,** maybe?

In short, every color is fine, except for that **TEDDY BEAR PAJAMA PATTERN.** That is not really appropriate for a superhero!

A final note, be careful with costumes such as **SWIMSUITS...** Even superheroes can catch **SUPERCOLDS!**

Some superheroes choose to wear **A MASK**.

If you choose to wear one, you could try a **FULL FACE MASK.**

OR A DOMINO ONE, to cover just your eyes.

What about a **VISOR?** A visor could be cool!

A **HOOD?**
Always looks good with a cape.

A **HELMET?** Well, it's a safe choice.

And what about **BUNNY EARS?** I wouldn't recommend them...
Not unless you want to look like **THE EASTER BUNNY.**

Costumes are cool and all, but now it's time to choose your...
SUPERPOWER

Will you be **SUPER STRONG?**

Or **SUPER FAST?**

Or perhaps you'd prefer to be **INVISIBLE?**

Will you be a **FLYING** superhero?

Or maybe one that **SHRINKS AND GROWS?**

MAKING FIRE OR ICE are popular choices.

What about **SHAPESHIFTING?**

Maybe **CONTROLLING THE WEATHER** is more your thing?
EVERYTHING IS POSSIBLE!

SECRET ORIGINS

This is the only thing you can't actually choose. It's something that **ALREADY HAPPENED.** Right?

Maybe your parents were **FROM ANOTHER PLANET** and sent you to Earth before that planet **BLEW UP.**

Perhaps you were hit by **COSMIC RAYS...**

Or were bitten by a **RADIOACTIVE INSECT.**

PETS AND SIDEKICKS

Sometimes superheroes need help to defeat supervillains. Having a **PARTNER OR PET** on board could be very useful.

Your little sister? Well, maybe not ideal!!

A pet should be able to follow you wherever you go. **A DOG** or **A CROW,** for example.

A CAT might not make the most cooperative of sidekicks.

A TURTLE, while cute, may not be the best choice to help you to quickly save the day!

And a **GOLDFISH**... Well, it's a goldfish! It lives in a bowl. If it doesn't have any **TELEKINETIC** superpowers, I'd pass!

SUPERTEAMS

Did you know you can also form a **TRIO** of superheroes?

Or a **QUARTET?**

But if you want to, you can have all your friends on your **SUPERTEAM!**

TRANSPORT

Not every superhero can fly, but never fear, there are lots of other options to get you where you want to go in the **NICK OF TIME!**

You may like a **CUSTOM SCOOTER**...

Or a **SUPER COOL MOTORBIKE!**

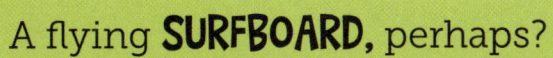

A flying **SURFBOARD,** perhaps?

What about a **SPECIAL FLYING CAR?**

Or any **FLYING OBJECT** for that matter. It's your choice.

HEADQUARTERS

Every professional superhero needs a **HEADQUARTERS**.

It could be a **SECRET BASE,** but it could also be a **HUGE PUBLIC BUILDING.**

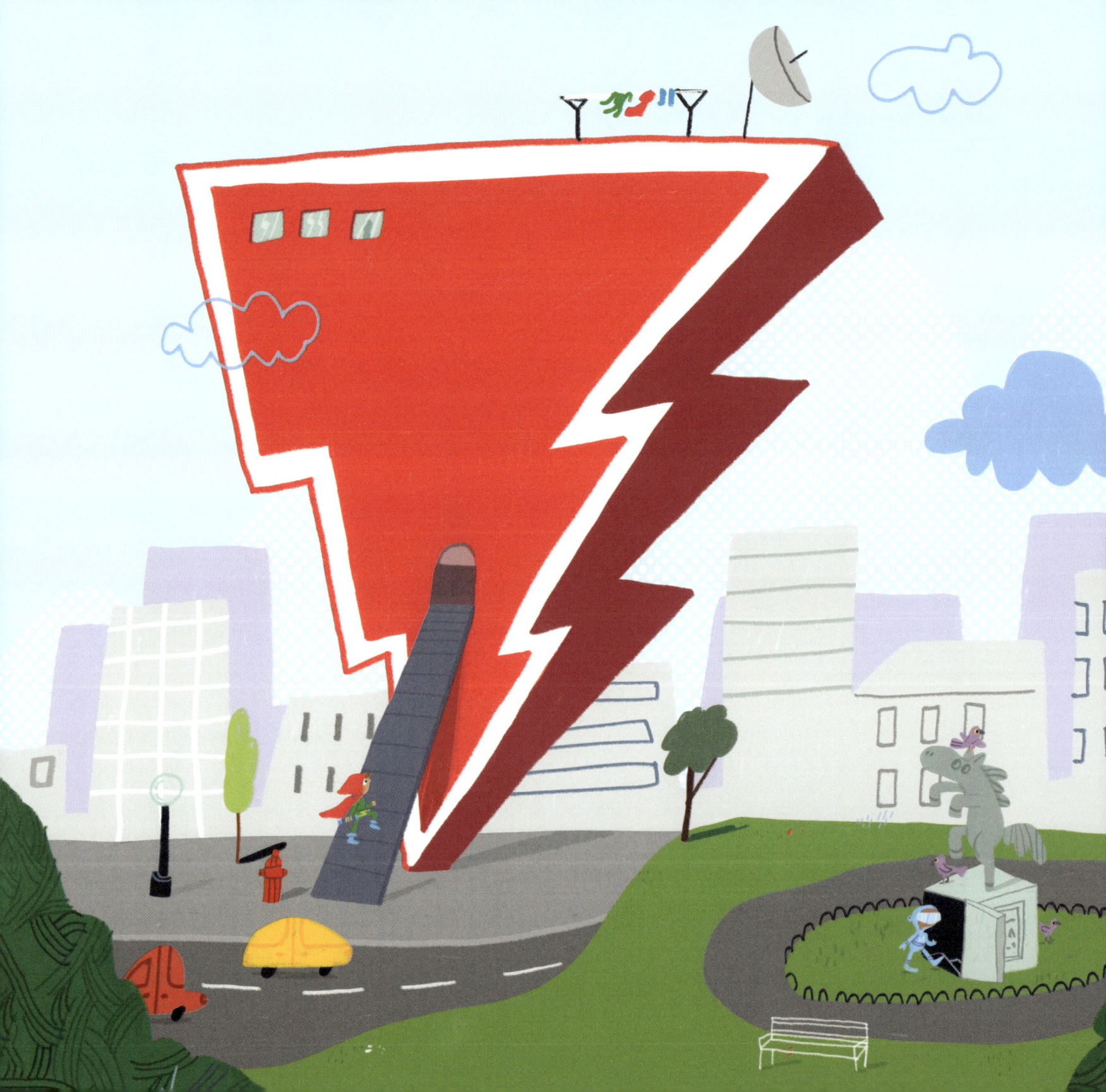

You may prefer something more sinister, like **A CAVE.**

If you can't afford one of these super hideouts, **YOUR ROOM** will do nicely. Just remember to put a sign on the door when you're doing superhero stuff.

Everything ready?

COSTUME

MASK

SUPERPOWER

PETS AND SIDEKICKS

TRANSPORT

HEADQUARTERS.

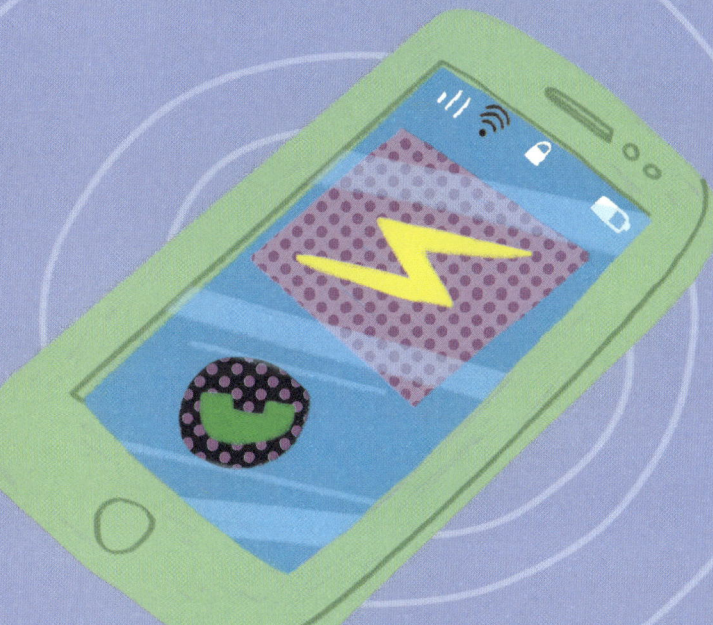

It's time for your
FIRST MISSION!

Will it be helping an **OLD GRANNY** cross the street?

Or preventing **A TERRIBLE TRAIN ACCIDENT?**

Maybe something harder like stopping
A FALLING METEORITE?

Or foiling **A BANK ROBBERY?**

Or even better, helping to fight...

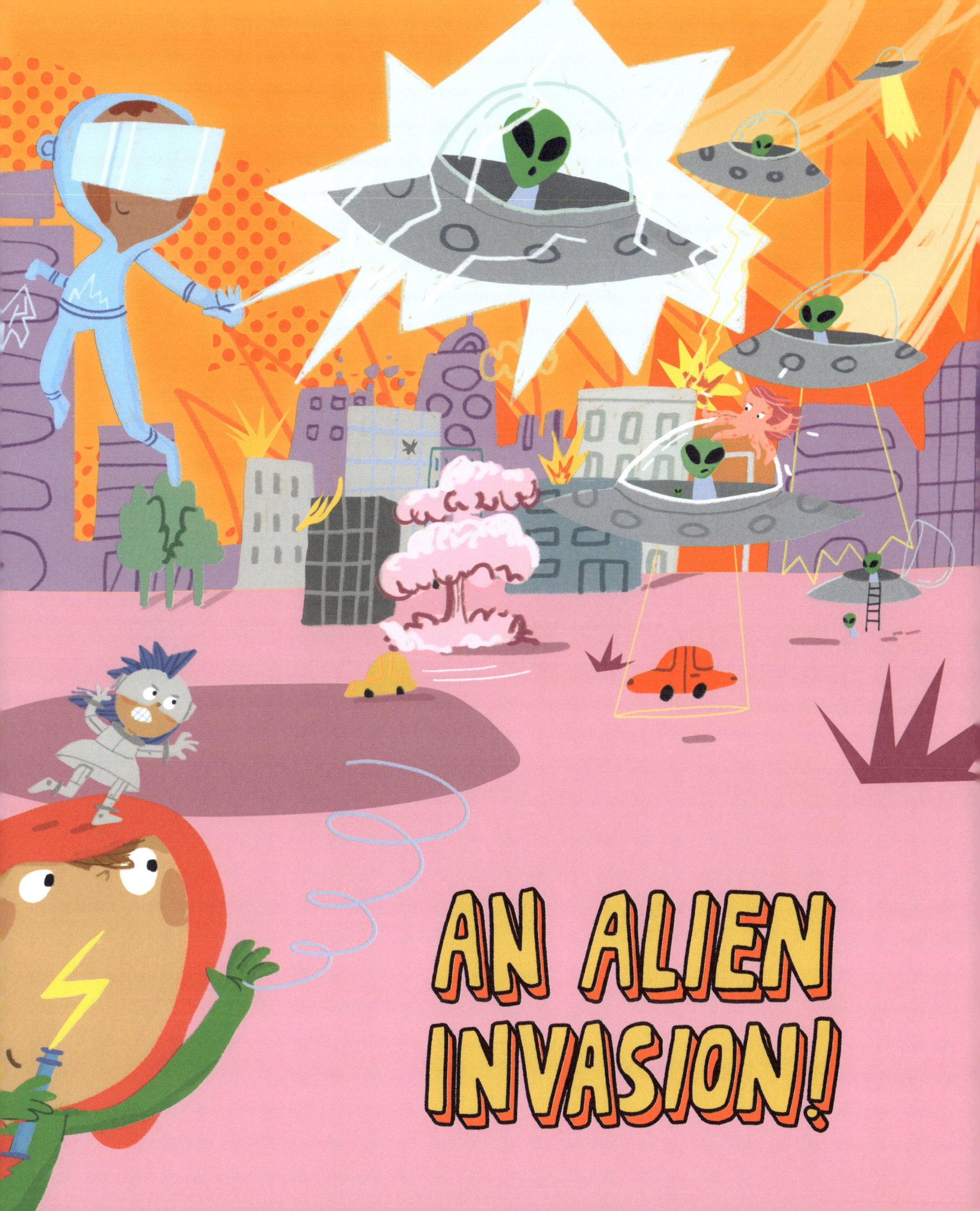

But of course you can't learn all of this in **JUST ONE DAY...**

To **KEEP LEARNING,** superheroes have to go to...